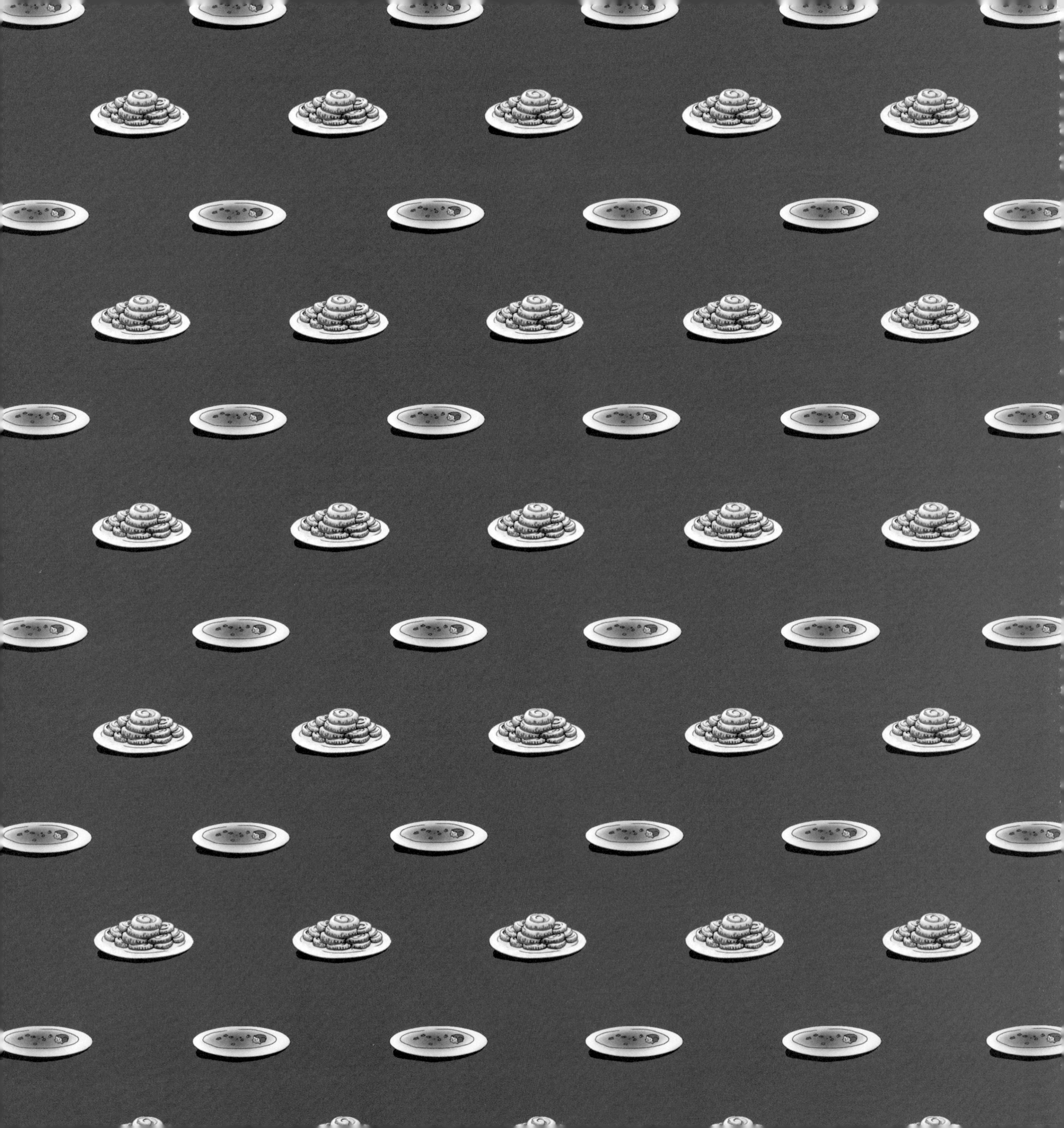

HUNGRY JOHNNY

 For information, write to the Minnesota Historical Society Press, 345 Kellogg Blvd. W., St. Paul, MN 55102-1906.

www.mhspress.org
The Minnesota Historical Society Press is a member of the Association of American University Presses.
Manufactured in Canada.
10 9 8 7 6 5 4 3 2 1
∞ The paper used in this publication meets the minimum requirements of the American National Standard for Information Sciences—Permanence for Printed Library Materials, ANSI Z39.48-1984.

International Standard Book Number
ISBN: 978-0-87351-926-7 (cloth)

LIBRARY OF CONGRESS CATALOGING-IN-PUBLICATION DATA

Minnema, Cheryl, 1973-
Hungry Johnny / Cheryl Minnema, Wesley Ballinger.
pages cm
Summary: "At the community feast, observing the bounty of festive foods and counting the numerous elders yet to be seated, Johnny learns to be patient and respectful despite his growling tummy"— Provided by publisher.
ISBN 978-0-87351-926-7 (cloth : alk. paper)
1. Ojibwa Indians—Minnesota—Juvenile fiction. [1. Ojibwa Indians—Fiction. 2. Indians of North America—Minnesota—Fiction. 3. Dinners and dining—Fiction. 4. Patience—Fiction. 5. Hunger—Fiction.] I. Ballinger, Wesley, illustrator. II. Title.
PZ7.M659Hu 2014
[E]—dc23
2013050241

Bekaa: Wait

Akwe niwii Miigwech: First I'd like to thank . . .

Wiisinig!: Eat!

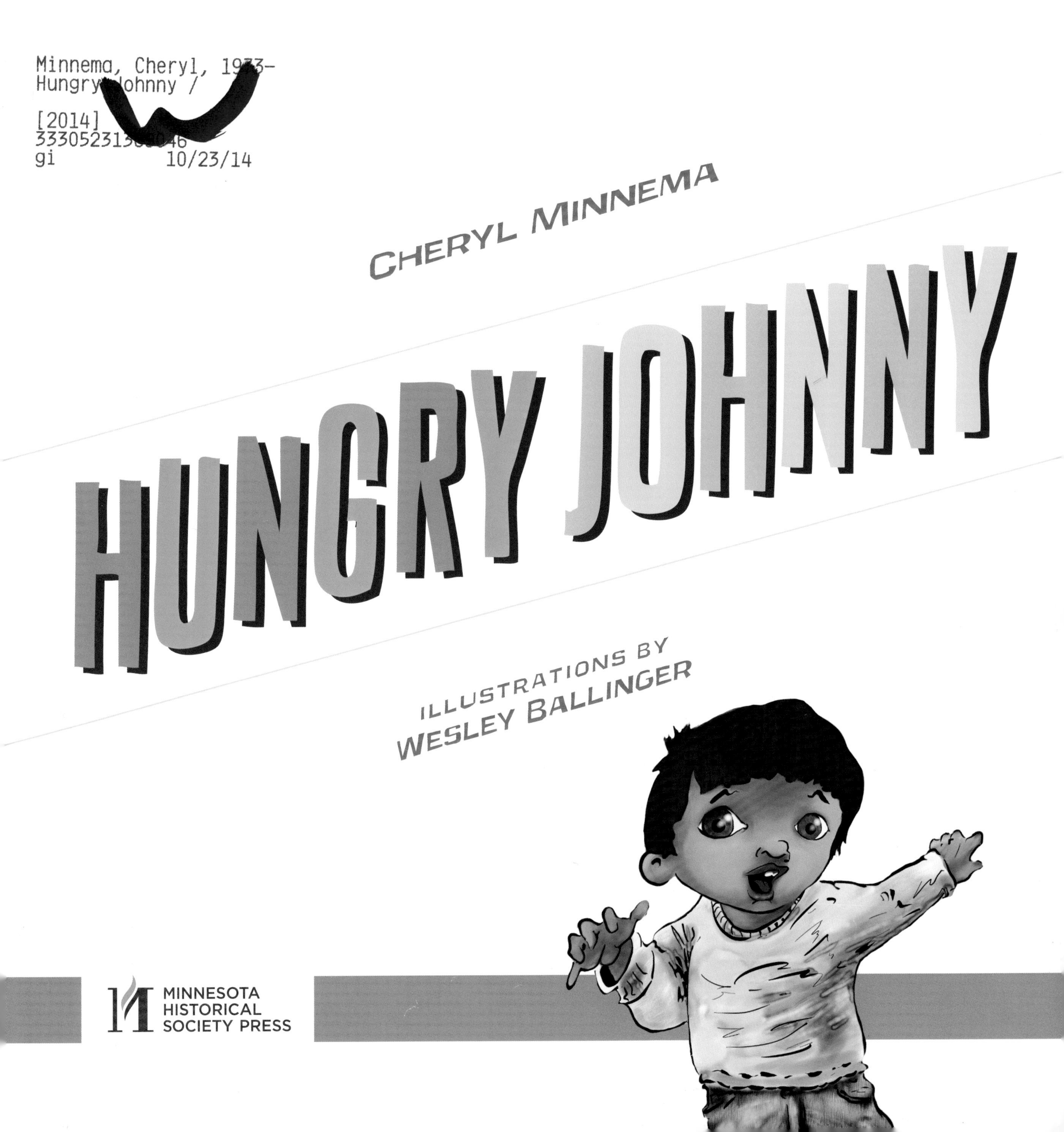

Cheryl Minnema

Hungry Johnny

Illustrations by Wesley Ballinger

Minnesota Historical Society Press

FOR
JOHNNY
BUBBA

Johnny was in
his snow fort
when his tummy
began to growl.

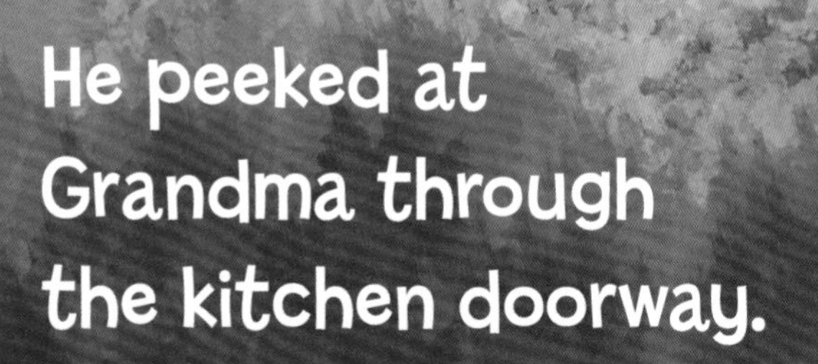

He peeked at Grandma through the kitchen doorway.

"I like to **EAT, EAT, EAT,**" said Johnny.

Grandma kept
on stirring and
stirring her kettle
of wild rice.

Johnny trotted into the kitchen,
straight for the apples, oranges, bananas,
and the new package of sweet rolls.

"I like to **EAT**, **EAT**, **EAT**," said Johnny.

Grandma shooed his hand away.

"**Bekaa**, these are for the community feast."

Johnny put his head down and started to drag his boots out of the kitchen.

"That means I will be waiting forever, and I'm **SO** hungry."

"But we are almost ready to go," said Grandma.

"Yay!" said Johnny, jumping up and down.

Grandma kept her eyes on the snowy dirt road.

Johnny sang, "I like to **EAT**, **EAT**, **EAT**. I like to **EAT**, **EAT**, **EAT**" all the way to the community center.

When the people were seated and the food neatly arranged, an elderly man began to say a very l-o-n-g prayer.

"Akwe niwii Miigwech ..."

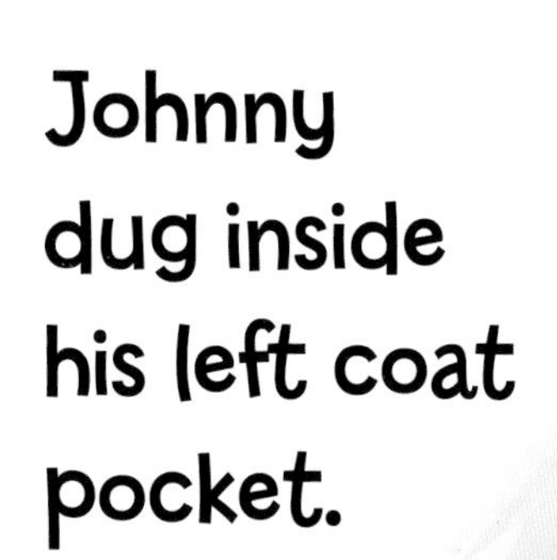

Johnny
dug inside
his left coat
pocket.

He pulled out
his mini-monster
truck, the
cartoon sticker
he got from
his five-year
check-up,
and the sparkly
white rock
he had found
in the driveway.

There were no snacks.

Then Johnny dug inside his pants pocket and pulled out his little plastic buddy.

"Big Bill," said Johnny, excited to have finally found him.

"Shhh," said Grandma.

Johnny put most of his treasures away and sat quietly until he heard the prayer end: “**Wiisinig!**”

Johnny stood up and said,
"It's time to **EAT**, **EAT**, **EAT**!"

Grandma gently tugged the sleeve of his sweater.

"**Bekaa**, we let the elders eat first."

Johnny sat down, "Why do elders get the good food first?" he asked.

"Out of respect," said Grandma.

"Well, why aren't you getting up to eat?" asked Johnny.

"Because I'm only a baby elder," said Grandma.

"What is a baby elder?" asked Johnny.

"It's when you are too young to be old and too old to be young," said Grandma.

"Huh?" asked Johnny.

Grandma laughed.

Johnny's tummy growled.

The long table filled.

"Grandma, I'm hungry," said Johnny.

Her soft hand patted his knee. "**Bekaa.**"

Johnny's mouth watered as he watched the elders eat fried potatoes, wild rice, goulash, big chunks of fry bread, and thickly frosted sweet rolls.

A place for two finally opened up at the table.

Johnny stood up and then sat back down.

“Already taken,” said Johnny.

He looked at all the people
still waiting to eat and
started to count them.
"One, two, three ..."

Grandma tapped
Johnny's knee.
"It's time to eat."

Johnny hopped up and trotted to the table. In a deep voice he said, “I like to **EAT**, **EAT**, **EAT**. I like to **EAT**, **EAT**, **EAT**.”

When Johnny sat down, the platter of frosted sweet rolls was empty!

"Ah, man," pouted Johnny.

A woman picked up the empty platter and put an even bigger platter of sweet rolls on the table.

"Eat up!" said the woman.

"**FINALLY**,"
said Johnny.

But then he saw Grandma's friend Katherine walk through the door.

Johnny looked down at his waiting plate and then back at Grandma's neighbor.

She was definitely not a baby elder.

Johnny
stood up
on his chair and yelled,
"Katherine, Katherine,
it's time to
EAT, EAT, EAT."

Johnny hopped
off the chair and
pulled it out.

When Katherine sat down, she patted her knee.

Johnny hopped onto her lap.

Grandma leaned over and whispered into Johnny's ear. "Why do the little boys get all the good food?"

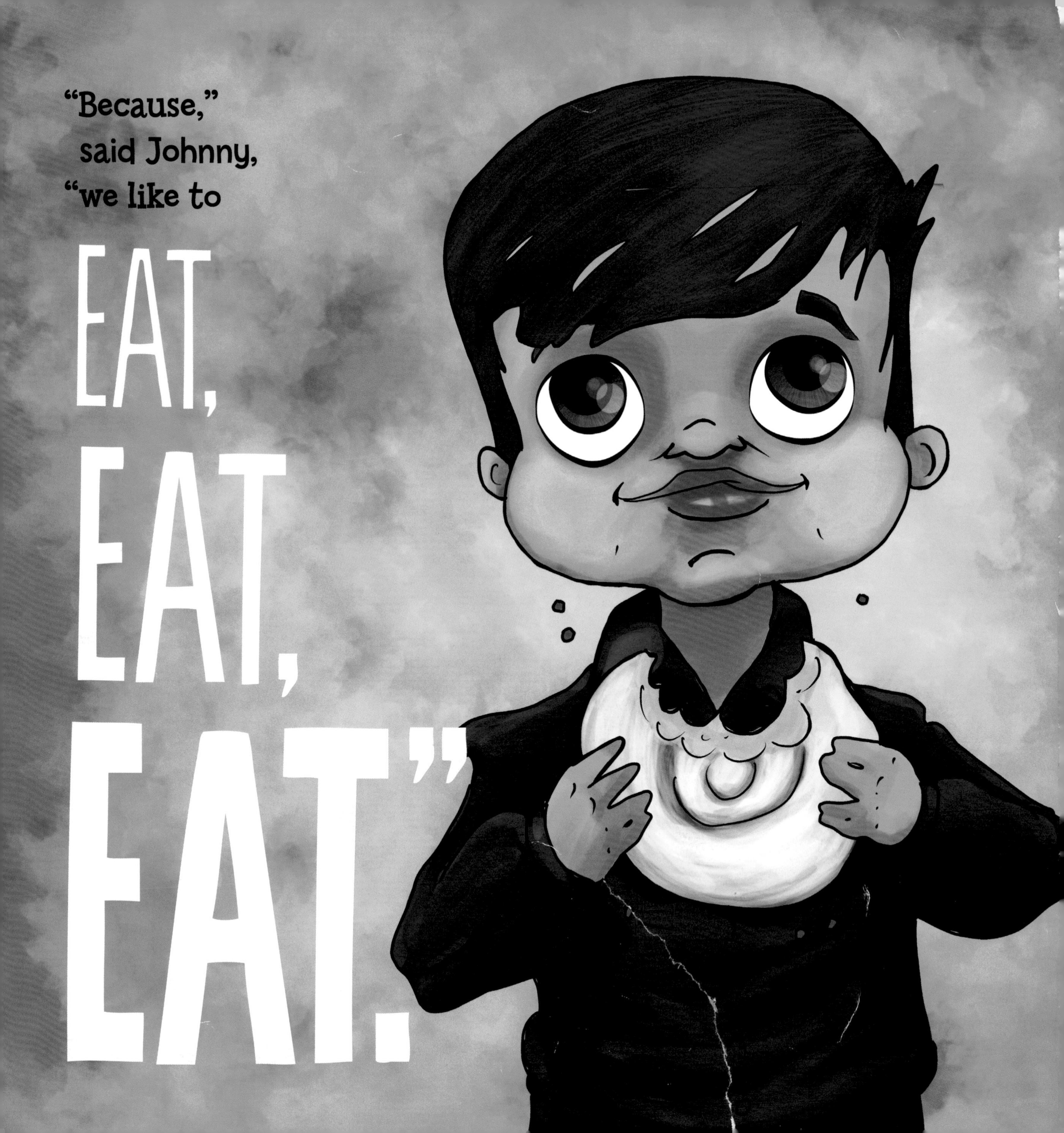
"Because,"
said Johnny,
"we like to
EAT,
EAT,
EAT."